OILI TANNINEN

Button &
Popper

Thames & Hudson

Publisher's Note

There are certain books that are simply astounding,
where the clarity of design and brilliance of color seem
to jump out and communicate on first reading the joy
of their creation. Such is the case with this book, the
mesmerizing work of Oili Tanninen, rightly renowned
in her native Finland. It's a privilege and a delight to
bring this magnificent work back into the hands of
children everywhere for the first time in over fifty years,
and for the first time ever in English. Some things
really do stand the test of time, as *Button & Popper*
is even more fresh and pertinent today than it was
on first publication. We thank Oili Tanninen for her
wonderful work and for enabling us to bring it to a new
generation of readers.

Roger Thorp

Foreword

Fall 1963. In a little village in central Finland.

We had returned from a foreign country after a
long time working abroad and were staying with
my parents-in-law and hunting for an apartment
in Helsinki. To find one was more difficult than we
had thought. It looked like nobody was ready to rent
anything to a family with two children. It was not
true, of course, but the irritation gave me the impulse
to do this book.

I wanted to make a happy book from this unpleasant
subject. So I chose fresh, pure colors. I wanted the
book to be cheap to print and buy. So I used only three
inks. And I gave it a very happy ending, of course.
Looking at the pictures now, 55 years later, I remember
the delightful scents that filled my studio as I was
working. My parents-in-law had foraged wild berries
and mushrooms in the woods and were preserving
them for the winter.

Critics in the newspapers liked what they saw and read.
"A modern touch," wrote one. Even the people who
were selecting books for the Hans Christian Andersen
Award chose my story for their honor list. Meanwhile,
we too found a little apartment—a good place to think
up many new stories with happy endings.

Oili Tanninen, 2019

The pixie family is made up of Mother, Father, and their
12 children. Imagine getting them all in this picture—it
was a palaver, believe me!

The pixie family lived in an apple tree. It was big and old and the apples that grew on it were the biggest and sweetest you could ever find.

The pixies were happy living in the apple tree. The children could climb its branches and eat as many apples as they wanted. Father sat at the foot of the tree, read the newspaper, and smoked his pipe. Mother baked apple pie and admired the drops of dew that settled on the red apples in the morning.

But winter was coming. The leaves turned yellow and the apples ran out. It rained and the pixies were cold.

Father looked for a new winter home, but found nothing. Mother and Father grew worried. They knew how hard it was to find a home for such a large family.

That evening, Mother made a pie using the last of the apples.
No one spoke—which was very strange. There's usually a fair bit of
a noise in a pixie family. Now, the only thing everyone could think
about was the winter home they didn't have. They were all very sad.

Then Button had an idea. He nudged his brother
Popper and gave him a sign by wiggling his left ear.
Button understood straight away what that meant:
TOMORROW YOU AND ME WILL GO AND
FIND A NEW HOME. Button nodded and the
matter was decided.

They ate their apple pie and went to bed as soon
as they were told. During the night they dreamed
the same dreams; they were twins, you see.

The others were still asleep when Button and Popper set off the next morning. They left a note for Mother that read: GONE TO SEE ABOUT SOMETHING. Outside it was raining so Popper turned back and went to get Father's umbrella. Button found an apple on the ground. He put it in his pocket for later.

Popper noticed that a curtain was twitching in one of the mushroom houses. Miss Shelly the snail was peeping out. She got quite a shock, and developed a headache, when she saw Button and Popper. All day she fretted about where they might have been going so early in the morning. But Button and Popper marched on towards town.

When they arrived in town the rain let up. Most people were still asleep. The mayor was snoring so loudly his house jumped up and down. Button and Popper went to the market square.

"Excuse me, do you know of anyone who would rent us somewhere to live?" the pixies asked Mrs. Floaty, who was selling balloons. "There are twelve of us children." "Twelve children!" shrieked Mrs. Floaty, just managing to keep hold of her balloons.

"Twelve children!" shrieked everyone else the pixies asked, like Mr. Bleak and Mrs. Peony. Everyone explained kindly but firmly that surely nowhere could be found for such a large family.

Professor Prilli stood next to the fish stall and tried to remember what he had come for. He had been standing there for at least ten minutes, racking his brains.

Button and Popper felt depressed. They were hungry and tired.
The sun was now high in the sky and it seemed like they wouldn't
find anywhere to live.

Professor Prilli was the only person they hadn't asked yet.
In the pixies' view, he looked far too dignified for such a question.

Popper yawned and yawned. He spotted an empty basket on the
ground, just by his feet. It was the basket Mrs. Peony used to bring
her flowers to sell at the market. The pixies climbed in.

Popper yawned again and lay down inside the basket. Button got out the apple from his pocket. He began munching on it thoughtfully as Popper fell asleep.

Just then Professor Prilli approached Mrs. Peony's stall, carrying his own basket. It was just like the one Button and Popper were in. Except there was a fish in the professor's basket. He had bought it, being unable to remember anything else.

"Good day," said Mrs. Peony. "What'll it be?"

"Good day," answered the professor. "May I have three sunflowers?" He put his basket down on the ground, next to Mrs. Peony's.

"One dollar fifty. There we go," said Mrs. Peony, passing the sunflowers to Professor Prilli.

The professor paid for the flowers, lifted up the basket, and dawdled towards home contentedly. He would not have been so content had he known there was no fish in his basket, but rather two pixies. HE HAD TAKEN MRS. PEONY'S BASKET!

And what about the pixies? Button was surprised when the basket started to move all by itself. He tried to peer over the edge of the basket to see where they were going. But Popper just carried on sleeping, unaware of the free ride he was getting. Button pinched Popper's ear, pulled his nose and tickled him under his chin, but he still wouldn't wake up.

The basket stopped rocking. It was quite dark and cool around them. Button guessed they were now in the professor's cellar. He began to grow cold. Popper finally woke up. Before he could say anything, Button explained what had happened.

They climbed out of the basket but found the door was locked. There were tall shelves all around them, full of bottles of juice and jars of jam. The pixies were very hungry.

"We'll never get out of here," cried Popper.
"And we left Father's umbrella at the market," sniffed Button.

Then Button happened to glance up. He wiped his tears
away quickly, so he could see better. There was a small
opening where the ceiling and the wall met and a little ray
of light was shining through it. "Hurray!" Button shouted.
"Will we fit through there?" asked Popper, doubtfully.

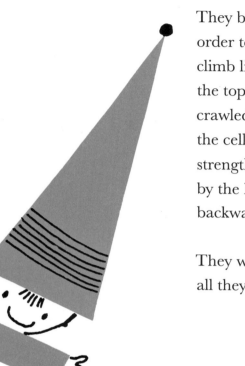

They began climbing up the shelves immediately in order to get to the opening. And they were able to climb like squirrels, you know. Soon they were on the top shelf, right below the opening. Button crawled through first and managed to get out of the cellar, with Popper pushing him with all his strength from behind. Then Button took Popper by the hands and pulled so hard that he fell backwards on to the ground.

They were outside! And they were so relieved, all they could do was laugh out loud.

"If only we could find a place like that!" the pixies said,
examining the professor's house. It was the finest house
they had ever seen.

"Now what do we do?" asked Popper. "Let's go back to the market to get Father's umbrella and the professor's basket of fish," Button explained.

The pixies ran to the square. There, Mrs. Peony clapped her hands in wonder, amazed at the story of the pixies' adventure. The basket of fish and the umbrella were exactly where they had left them.

PEPPER STREET

The pixies decided to take the basket of fish back to the professor. It was late in the afternoon now. They were disappointed their search for somewhere to live had come to nothing.

"Come in, the door's open," shouted the professor from his living room, when the pixies rang the bell.

"Who are you?" he asked in amazement, putting on his glasses. "Pixies! How interesting!" he exclaimed.

Button and Popper gave him his basket and explained how the switch had happened. "How interesting!" cried the professor again in wonder. "But tell me, why were you at the market this morning?" he asked.

"We were looking for somewhere to live, but we couldn't find anywhere. There are twelve of us children."

"Really," said the professor, full of interest. He began wiping
his glasses with a handkerchief. "Listen, tomorrow I'm going
on a research trip to the South Pole and I won't be back
until next spring. You could move in here," he suggested.

Button and Popper pricked up their ears, thinking they had misheard. "But there are twelve of us children," they reminded Professor Prilli again. "You won't disturb me, I'll be at the South Pole!" the professor laughed.

The pixies saw now that the professor meant it. They bowed as nicely as they could and said MANY THANKS and promised to water the professor's flowers. They were so excited they couldn't stay still for one more second. They ran all the way home.

Miss Shelly saw the pixies run past her window again,
and her headache worsened a little, because she
still didn't know where they'd been all day.

But in the apple tree, all twelve children let out a
great shout, when they heard the wonderful news.
Father sighed with relief and lit his pipe, then for the first
time in a long while he started reading the newspaper.

"It's the sort of thing that only happens in fairy tales,"
said Mother Pixie, but no one heard her. They were
all busy dreaming of their new home.

Button & Popper © Oili Tanninen, 1964
First published in Finnish as *Nappi ja Neppari* by Otava Publishing Company.
Published in the English language by Thames & Hudson Ltd, London by
arrangement with R&B Licensing AB

Foreword © 2019 Oili Tanninen
Publisher's note © 2019 Thames & Hudson Ltd, London
Translated by Emily Jeremiah

First published in the United States in 2019 by Thames & Hudson Inc., 500 Fifth
Avenue, New York, New York 10110

www.thamesandhudsonusa.com

Library of Congress Control Number 2019931887

ISBN 978-0-500-65201-5

Printed and bound in China by C&C Offset Printing Co. Ltd